Two Men and a Maiden

TWO MEN AND A MAIDEN

Winifred Foley

ISIS
LARGE PRINT
Oxford

First published in Great Britain 2007
by
ISIS Publishing Ltd.

Published in Large Print 2007 by ISIS Publishing Ltd.,
7 Centremead, Osney Mead, Oxford OX2 0ES
by arrangement with
the Author

British Library Cataloguing in Publication Data
Foley, Winifred
    Two men and a maiden. – Large print ed.
    1. Domestic fiction
    2. Large type books
    I. Title
    823.9'14 [F]

ISBN 978–0–7531–7970–3 (hb)
ISBN 978–0–7531–7971–0 (pb)

Printed and bound in Great Britain by
T. J. International Ltd., Padstow, Cornwall

To Chris, Richard, Nick and Jenny and their spouses
for being so good to me.

ACKNOWLEDGEMENT

I would like to thank my niece Elizabethann
for her help and advice.

CHAPTER
ONE

Laura was sixteen years old, and like many thousands of girls from working class homes she had gone into domestic service at the age of fourteen. She was now more able to deal with the trauma of homesickness. The headmaster of her village school had been upset that the brightest pupil he had ever taught had gone into the capped and aproned servitude of the domestic worker. But needs must when there is a family to support and there are children to be fed.

Laura's first job had been for a gentle impoverished aristocratic type of woman about sixty years old. The trouble was, she wanted to live by the standards of the well-to-do on a pauper's income. Thanks to her poverty, she rarely gave extra work to Laura by having guests to stay and economy was practised to its limits.

Miss Temple did the cooking herself and she always shared equally with Laura. For breakfast she cooked two rashers of streaky bacon and two pieces of fried bread. Then she cut off the rind of the bacon to flavour the penny packet of Maggi powdered soup that started the main meal of the day. The cheapest tinned salmon were never used straight from the tin; the fish was mixed with breadcrumbs, herbs, flour and an egg to make enough fish cakes for several dinners. Empty tea and sugar packets were opened out flat to ensure not a grain of sugar of leaf of tea was wasted.

When Laura had been there nearly two years, a serious sounding Miss Temple asked Laura to see her in the drawing room when she had finished washing up the breakfast dishes. Puzzled, Laura agreed. What had she done? Miss Temple did not seem cross with her, but to be asked into the drawing room and told to sit down meant it was something important. A flushed and troubled Miss Temple told Laura that the tithe bill for her church pew had gone up and also the rates on her house had increased. She lived on a small fixed income and could no longer afford to pay Laura five shillings a week: she could only manage three shillings and four pence. She had no complaints about Laura's work.

2

"Poor Papa! He invested the family's wealth badly and died before he could recoup matters," Miss Temple sighed, "If you stayed with me, I would give you my needlework box I had as a child. It is a beautiful box with a silver thimble, scissors and tape measure, and a sampler I did at six years old. My nanny said it was the best one any of her charges had ever done."

It was now Laura's turn to blush for Miss Temple and for herself, for she hardly knew how to answer. At one pound a month she was able to send a five-shilling postal order to her hard-up mother trying to cope bringing up her younger siblings on her father's inadequate wages. The rest she really needed for herself — to pay sixpence for the cheapest seat at the little theatre on her half day off, tuppence for humbugs to assuage her hunger between mealtimes, saving for her annual two weeks' holiday, and buying clothes and shoes. Her mother's need was greater than Miss Temple's. After all, Miss Temple was fit enough to do her own work, she did not really need a maid, it was just silly pride because she had been brought up in a household with four servants and a nanny. All the same, she felt sorry for her mistress; it must be awful to be lonely and economically strained as well.

"I'm afraid I cannot work for those wages, Miss Temple," Laura finally replied. "It would mean I couldn't help my mother at all." She added, "But I am willing to work for the lower wage whilst I stay for my month's notice to give you time to get someone else."

"Thank you, Laura," Miss Temple replied, "I will give you a good reference, and I know I shan't get a girl as good as you for such a low wage."

When the month was up and they said their goodbyes, there was a glint of tears in both pairs of eyes.

CHAPTER
TWO

How lovely it was for Laura to be back with her family, to lie in bed late in the morning, to be treated as someone special and to play hopscotch and skip and run wild in the woods with her brothers and sisters and younger village friends! But Laura knew it must not be for long. She must get another job so as not to be a burden to her parents. She borrowed a newspaper from their elderly neighbour and saw an advert for a general maid in Aldgate, London, for ten shillings a week, all found: twice what she had been getting. She wrote for the job, enclosing her references from the school and Miss Temple. She got a reply by return and a one-pound postal order, which more than covered her train fare to Paddington. She was slightly surprised that the advertiser did not wish to see her before hiring her, and that the letter asked that she should not come on a Friday or Saturday, whereas Sunday would be quite acceptable. However, the chance was too good and she wrote back at once, saying what day she would arrive.

London! It was such an awfully long way off. The teacher at school often told them about London: its grandeur, its slums, the great and clever people who had trod its pavements! Just to live there must make one somebody special. On the day of departure, Laura was a mixture of anticipation and apprehension. Her heart felt heavier than her belongings as the station came into view. London was such a long way off and it would take a year to earn the two weeks' holiday. She was glad she had kept enough pennies to buy her mam and the younger children a penny bar of chocolate each from the vending machine on the little station halt platform, but there were tears in everybody's eyes when they waved goodbye.

As the train ate up the miles Laura could not believe England was so big. But at long last the countryside gave way to housing, miles of houses; she even began to wonder whether the train had passed Paddington Station by mistake. She looked up at the back view of the tall buildings along the railway with amazement at their height until the train puffed to a halt. Laura had not seen the entrance to the station she was in: this vast roofed place with rows of rail tracks, some with trains on them — it was obviously a terminal — this then was Paddington Station, and Laura felt scared. How on earth was she going to find her way to number 9 Leman Street, Aldgate? As she boarded the train at the little halt in the Forest, she had felt quite important, especially with the case she had bought to replace the battered old tin trunk: it had cost two shillings and eleven pence and was made of strong cardboard, polished brown to look like leather. Now she felt as insignificant as a fly in a jam pot. Her lip had begun to quiver and a tear was gathering in her eye, when a brisk young woman approached her.

"Are you Laura Bailey that's come to work for the Cohens in Leman Street, Aldgate?" she asked.

"Oh yes, that's me, and am I glad to see you!" replied a relieved Laura.

"My name's Dolly. I work for some friends of theirs. They asked me to meet you. You knows it's Jews you will be working for?" she continued. No, Laura did not know. "Well, don't worry; they're all right, not snobby-nosed sods like our lot. And you don't have to wear caps and aprons. Burn your bloody caps if you've brought them. I hate them!" she continued vehemently. "They got some feelings for you, but mind you, they'll try to sell you some bargains to get your wages back. Just say "no"! They don't mind. Oh, and if you don't ask for them, they won't give you your half days off," she added helpfully. "Come on then, we'll go by Underground, it's quicker."

Wide-eyed and open-mouthed, Laura followed Dolly down the incredible moving stairs to the busy Underground, amazed and impressed by Dolly's sophistication in using these marvels. On arriving at Aldgate, she was glad to be back up on the pavement, back to a world so unbelievably different from the one she had left. She gazed at rows of identical tall houses with not so much as a blade of grass to be seen. It was majestically awful. After a short walk Dolly stopped by one of the houses, pulled a key on a string through the letterbox, and opened the door into a long passage with a staircase leading upwards in front of them. and a stair at the end of the passage, going down to a basement.

"Here she is! Here's your shiksa, Mrs. Cohen," Dolly called down just as a very pretty Jewish girl about twelve years old came up the stairs.

"Momma says do you want a cup of tea?" she asked Dolly.

"No, thanks. This is supposed to be my half-day off. I'm off!" Dolly replied as she rushed through the door.

The little girl, whose name was Rachel, immediately reminded Laura of the sisters she had left behind, and the tears stung her eyes again. Rachel turned and led her down the stairs into what Laura thought to be a very large kitchen. It was quite light as the basement window was big, and it was papered in a light cream with a small pattern on it. There was a range, a dresser and a huge table around which sat Rachel's two single brothers who lived at home, two married brothers with their wives, and a cousin, for Momma Cohen was never happier than when cooking and dishing up food. Altogether nine pairs of brown eyes gazed at Laura as room was made for her to sit at the table. Momma Cohen was a rather stout, bent handsome Jewess in her early fifties. Poppa Cohen was away in a Jewish nursing home in Hove to avoid the worst of the winter fogs.

During her whole time with the Cohens, it was the only meal Laura would eat with the family. Momma Cohen could not bear to see food wasted, so Laura was always given jobs to do whilst the family ate their meals, then the leavings were dished up to her, except for breakfast. The family also had a married daughter, Fanny, and a single daughter, Leah who lived at home and was engaged to be married.

The house was a four-storied tenement. The basement housed the kitchen/scullery/dining room and a room with two beds, which Laura was to share with Rachel. On the ground floor was an enormous sitting room, that was never used, containing a sumptuous brown leather three-piece suite on which were large pink velvet cushions. On this floor was also the huge master bedroom for Momma and Poppa and a large entrance hall. The next floor had three bedrooms, for Leah, Adam and David. David was the most important member of the clan as he was the family's breadwinner, their father being too ill to work.

Level with the ground floor was a large, partly covered yard, which housed the wash copper and a bench with several zinc tubs. There was an outside tap and a flush toilet. There was a second toilet on a landing but no sign of a bathroom. The lack of a bathroom was overcome every Thursday evening when all the family and Laura went down to the public baths for their weekly ablutions and hair wash. Laura loved this break but was sad it cost her tuppence for the bath, a penny each for two towels and a penny for a small tablet of soap and a penny tip for the woman who controlled the water flow to give some extra water. She also bought to take with her a three-penny packet of Amami shampoo powder, which meant spending nine pence a week from her ten-shilling wages.

The top floor was the factory and the office, where David employed his sister, four brothers, one brother-in-law and a cousin, making fur collars and cuffs for coats: a very popular fashion of that era. David had worked spare time in his schooldays for a furrier and as soon as he left school he went to work for him. By the time he was nineteen, with his intelligence, persuasive powers and determination, he had borrowed enough capital to start business on his own. It had flourished and brought in a good living for most of his family. They all looked up to David, especially his parents, who had begun to fret that at thirty-one years old David was not married. Leah was engaged, his younger brother Adam was seeing a nice Jewish girl on a serious footing, but David was too wrapped up in business to be hurried.

When Laura had arrived at the Cohens, she was a five-foot six-inch girl with long straight hair and a beautiful face that had never known lipstick or powder. She was pale from two years of inadequate food, and life with Miss Temple had somewhat dulled her confidence and personality. A few months of Momma Cohen's cooking transformed her into a nubile beauty of more than average intelligence. Only her hands detracted from her physical symmetry, for they were rough, red and swollen. Listening to, and gradually sharing in, the lively talk of the Cohens, she often impressed them. On occasions it gave her confidence to speak up on her own behalf.

She knew and made no demur about eating what the family did not want, such as bread rolls, cake and fruit, etc., but she noticed how unappetising her dinners were. One washing day, she watched from the yard what happened when the family went back upstairs to work. As she suspected, the leftover leavings on their plates were scraped on to one plate and put in the oven for her. When she was called down to the kitchen for dinner, and the plate was put in front of her, she pushed it away and said, "I don't want that dinner."

12

"For vy? Vot you mean, you don't vont your dinner?" Momma Cohen asked, shocked.

"I don't want the scrapings off your children's plates," Laura answered. "If you don't think I have earned some food straight from the saucepan, then I'd rather go without. And I know it was off their plates since I saw you do it through the window. Why can't you leave some in the saucepan for me?" Laura asked. From then on, the practice stopped.

She also laughingly questioned why during the hours of Shabbat no-one was allowed to switch on any gas or electricity: she was told it was considered a sin. Laura answered that electricity had not been invented when the Bible was written, but she ran around switching the lights on for them, and lighting the gas stove for Momma. She also had to polish the huge copper samovar, fill it with water and bring it to the boil for them to make their countless cups of lemon tea during Shabbat. "And what about my soul," she would giggle, "committing all these sins over the Sabbath?"

Over the months an almost sisterly relationship grew between Rachel and Laura. When Laura's jobs were finished in the evening and Rachel had done her homework, they would go outside and play ball, hop scotch or skipping on the pavement. When one day Rachel's homework was art, the teacher had told her to draw an action picture. Laura had been the top scholar at art lessons in her village school and offered to help. She got Rachel to stand in a running pose in her school uniform, sketched her, and Rachel delivered it as her own work. At school, the teacher was so impressed with Rachel's new talent that a seat was put out for her in the schoolyard, and the materials for her to sketch what she could see. Poor Rachel, "Oh what an awful web we weave when once we practise to deceive" sat very aptly on her plight. She was in disgrace at the end of the afternoon. Laura was truly sorry: she often helped Rachel with her homework but from then on she would be very careful.

Rachel's company meant that Laura sometimes enjoyed a bit of her lost childhood and Laura's company helped Rachel, for Momma began to worry about Rachel starting to menstruate. Like many mothers, she did not relish telling Rachel the facts of life. Instead, she asked Laura if she would tell Rachel what to expect. To be trusted with this task touched and pleased Laura. Just over a week later Rachel shyly approached Laura to tell her she had started bleeding.

From six-thirty in the morning until the washing up was done from the early evening meal, Laura was kept busy. Each day had its burden of chores to get through to Momma's very high standards. Monday was washing day, up at 6.30, first clean the kitchen range and light the fire, then up to the backyard to fill the copper from the yard tap and light the fire beneath it. By then, Momma was dressed and she would give Laura the money to fetch a bag of freshly ground coffee and newly baked crusty bread rolls, as well as tuppence-worth of chloride of lime powder from the chandler's shop. This was mixed to a paste, then added to a large tub of cold water where all the whites were soaked for ten minutes before their last rinse under the running cold tap water. Even when the sheets and teacloths were becoming threadbare, they were as white as the day they were bought. In the winter, what with rubbing all the clothes down on the washing board in hot soapy soda water and then the rinsing in freezing cold water, by the time the washing was mangled, Laura's hands, already badly chapped, would be bleeding, and there was still the gas stove in the scullery to be taken to pieces and scrubbed with hot water from the copper.

One washday evening, David came down the basement stairs as Laura was scrubbing the scullery floor and he noticed her hands were bleeding. He sent Rachel up to the office first aid box for a tin of ointment and a roll of bandage. He scolded Momma and set about himself smoothing Laura's hands in Zambuk ointment and bandaging them. Though neither of them knew it, Cupid had poked his nose in the deed. Laura was astounded at his kindly action and he was astounded at how angry he felt at Laura's treatment. Afterwards he chided himself for the thoughts of her that came into his head. It was unthinkable that he, a thirty-one year old Jew, should fall in love with a seventeen-year old penniless shiksa. Laura scolded herself for becoming so impressed by his kindly action and falling for the expression in his big soft brown eyes. Before she went to bed, Rachel rubbed more ointment thickly on Laura's hand, then she would put on an old pair of white cotton gloves to heal her hands somewhat by morning.

Tuesday's tasks included turning out the bedrooms, stripping the beds down to the iron frames and painting them with spirits of salt to try to keep the bugs off the beds. It did not always work. No matter how much housework was done, the bugs came out of the walls at night. Sometimes Rachel would challenge Laura which bug out of two would climb to the ceiling first. All too often the exhausted Laura would be fast asleep before any insect reached the ceiling. Whilst the family ate their breakfast, Laura would clean the front steps and polish the brass knocker and mop and polish the hallway.

As soon as the family went upstairs to work, Momma would call her down to breakfast. How Laura enjoyed it! Momma poured boiling water over the coffee on the side of the range, then boiled a saucepan of milk to add to the strained coffee. With a couple of spoons of sugar, the coffee was like nectar to the hungry Laura. With a generous plate of scrambled eggs and as many buttered crusty rolls as she could eat, Laura was ready to tackle all her jobs in good spirits. Sometimes Momma would tell Laura about her peasant girlhood in Poland. They could not afford soap to do the washing. Instead, every couple of months on a fine day they would take their washing in a handcart to the nearby river. To cleanse it they saved the ashes from the fire and put them in bags to beat the soiled washing spread out on boulders at the river's edge. It was very hard work but worked as well as the washing in the yard.

Momma had never worn a proper pair of shoes till she came to London to work long hours in an East End tailor's business. She had gone short of food as a youngster and now felt very rich indeed, being able to cook all she wanted for her family. On the evening of Shabbat, Momma did not cook. Instead Rachel and Laura went to Blooms' famous boiled salt beef restaurant for sandwiches. The aroma as they waited was mouth-watering. Friday evening supper never left any sandwiches for Laura, and though she was given something to eat she always felt a hunger that evening for a salt-beef sandwich.

Sometimes on these evenings a wave of homesickness would engulf Laura. She would compare Leman Street, Aldgate, with her beloved Forest of Dean. Here, rows of grim, tall, grey tenements and grey, dusty pavements replaced the beauty of huge oak trees and woodland paths. There, in their seasons, bluebells, foxgloves, daffodils and other wild flowers provided a feast of colour and beauty for the eye under a wide spread sky. Here the colour came from goods and clothes in the shops. In the

Forest, each season brought its loveliness: the delicate budding of green in spring, the long hours of sunshine in summer to play in what was a natural paradise for children, with trees to climb, pools to paddle in, grassy banks for games, etc. Autumn made even the most insensitive stand and stare at its glorious colours. Winter brought its own décor with the magic of snow. The seasons also brought their tribulations: shortage of water, chilblains, candle-lit darkness, shortage of work, illness and hunger. Here in London, water came from a tap, light at the flick of a switch. She had plenty to eat in London too. It was all wonderful, except on the days when London suffered its pea-soup fogs, sulphuric black blanketing the city, crushing the spirit and punctuating everything with coughs and sighs. The fogs made the cleaning on Wednesdays of all the windows except those of the factory a very hard day for Laura.

Thursday was another very busy day, when Momma took two baskets and four large bags to do the shopping for the Jewish weekend. At about 9am she would set off, telling Laura to come and meet her in Petticoat Lane in an hour and a half's time: Momma did not want Laura to waste any time. She was friendly with the woman on a salt fish stall, who would keep an eye on her baskets and bags as she filled them one by one, and left them behind the stall. Momma was a fussy shopper, poking the chickens for the plumpest breasts, wanting her fruits from the front of the stalls and bargaining the prices.

Meantime, Laura made a start on the weekly turnout of the dining room. She would stack the eighteen bentwood chairs onto the table, then tackle the carpet which covered the floor, using a mixture of damp tea-leaves saved for the job and a half bar of salt. Both were sprinkled liberally on the carpet, then brushed off with a hard bristled brush and dustpan until every tea-leaf had been picked up. It took the dust up but had gradually turned the patterned carpet to a faded brown. Then the big black fireplace, which never had a fire lit in it, had to be polished. Then the chairs were polished and put back round the table. Then it was time for the weekly coating of London dust to come off the sideboard. A bucket of hot soda and soapy water was used to wash all the paintwork. The window was cleaned last of all. There was lots of silverware on the sideboard: many candlesticks and dishes. These would have to be done in the evening after they returned from their baths, on newspapers spread on the kitchen table. Luckily for Laura, Momma could not read and did not notice Laura used her weekly tuppenny treat of *The Filmgoer* so she could read as she polished. Rachel knew, but Rachel was very fond of Laura.

When the hour and a half was up, Laura took off her apron and walked to Petticoat Lane. She loved it — the bustle, noise and colour, especially when she saw the tall black man with coloured feathers round his head selling racing tips in sealed envelopes. He called himself "Prince Monolulu" and Laura wondered why he bothered to sell tips: if they were any good he could make a fortune following them himself. Momma would be waiting by the fish stall surrounded with her shopping bounty. Laura carried two loaded bags in each hand and Momma struggled home with the baskets.

On Shabbat Laura was kept busy because of the constant daylong stream of family, friends and relatives that called in at the Cohens, all eating their heads off. Among the favourite goodies were a mixture of chopped liver, hard-boiled eggs and fried onions spread on matzos biscuits. There were pickled herrings, borsch and chicken soup and Momma's special chocolate marbled cake and strudel, with countless cups of lemon tea. Laura did an endless job of washing up. Most of the guests stayed over four hours on a Saturday so they could enjoy both the meat and milk dishes.

A half-day off was never mentioned, but here Rachel came to her aid. Rachel had been conceived when her mother was forty-two and her father more than a decade older. An unexpected latecomer, she was a beautiful baby and utterly adored by all the family. She was hardly ever refused anything. Rachel would ask Laura when she wanted to go to the pictures, then say to her mother she wanted to see the film if Laura would come with her. At seventeen with no hope of a boyfriend, Laura would daydream romances with the current film hero. The picture-house was the Brick Lane Palace, a squalid little cinema with a carpet of orange peel, sweet wrappers and peanut shells, and where most of the seats cost sixpence.

Laura particularly remembered one evening at the pictures. Despite Rachel warning her that Leah could sell a side of bacon to a Rabbi, Laura had parted with some of her wages for a pair of high-heeled shoes Leah had sold her. Alas, they were a size and a half too small. By the time they got to the cinema Laura's feet were swollen and she was tottering with pain. Oh, the relief of taking them off when they got their seats, and oh, the impossibility of getting them on again when the programme finished. She walked home bare-footed.

One Sunday evening Rachel took Laura by Underground to the City. In 1930 it had not been bombed and many of its streets were still narrow and cobbled. The few shops were tiny with bottle glass windows, mostly selling old prints or books. There was not a soul about and Laura was fascinated by the feeling of history that engulfed her. Had a girl appeared selling lavender in an old-fashioned bonnet and gown, she would not have been surprised.

One autumn evening Rachel said she wanted to take Laura to see the West End. They got on a number 15 bus and nothing had prepared Laura for the thrill of going down the incline to Piccadilly Circus. It was like fairyland with the statue of Eros in the centre and myriads of glittering lights: what a magic place London was! They got off the bus and went gazing at the shop windows, then stood stock still at the sight of a woman in one of the shadowy outskirts. She was painted up almost like a clown with red lips and cheeks and frizzed hair and wore a very tight skirt and very high-heeled shoes. They stood in shocked surprise and rudely stared open-mouthed at her until she snarled viciously at them to "Clear orf, or else . . ." Slightly scared they hurried off, only to see a couple of similar-looking women in other shadowy doorways.

"What a sight!" they giggled, "Whatever are they standing about like that for?" The two innocents were thoroughly intrigued.

The next excitement for Laura was when Rachel came home from school to say the end of the school year prize giving was on the next week and the Duchess of York, accompanied by the Duke, was going to present the prizes in the evening. All pupils could take a guest, and Rachel asked, "Can Laura come with me, please?" Poppa was still away and schools were foreign territory to Momma, so with David's permission, Laura had the privilege. The school was crowded; on a dais in the main hall a couple of sumptuous chairs for the royal behinds were placed in the front. There was a great buzz of conversation in the hall, which stopped at once as the headmaster ushered in the guests and some local dignities. Laura was surprised and disappointed by the appearance of the royal guests: they looked so plebeian despite the quality of their clothes. The Duchess seemed a short, almost dumpy little figure with a pleasant face set off by a dark fringe. She wore a blue hat and blue coat lavishly trimmed with fur and two rows of pearls, and the lights made flashes across the hall from her jewels. Laura wondered if the fur trim could possibly have been made at her house. But jewels and title or not, she just did not look how Laura had imagined a royal duchess should. She had expected someone tall and elegant who would stand out in a crowd. This one looked as though, if she wore ordinary clothes, she would not be noticed among the shoppers in Petticoat Lane. She even looked as though she might have wrinkles in her stockings. What did impress Laura were the prize-winning pupils in their smart uniforms. How she envied them and wished she were still at school. That night she dreamt she had been a pupil and the Duchess had given her a diamond necklace.

It was Momma who suggested Laura's next outing. At a hall near the synagogue there was going to be a jumble sale in the evening; maybe Laura would get some bargains. Laura took her wages and Rachel with her, and came away delighted with lots of clothes bargains, many for her mother who would now not have to worry about something tidy to wear to chapel. What a joy to pack the huge parcels to send home.

CHAPTER
THREE

She was nearly eighteen years old before the Cohens spared her for her overdue annual two weeks' holiday. Poppa Cohen had returned home, a frail, shrunken figure with a terrible chesty cough. Laura felt great pity for him and understood why he was now a very orthodox Jew.

Oh the joy to be home with her family and friends in the lovely Forest of Dean! To see the happiness on their faces when she took skipping ropes with proper handles out for her two younger sisters, packets of marbles for her brother, tobacco for Dad and a pretty flowered tablecloth for her mother. Her parents were proud of what a tall, well-built pretty girl she was now. She loved to be able to lie in as late as she liked in the morning, to be fussed over by her mother, to play hop scotch and skipping, to gather kindling wood with her siblings, and at odd times do a little mild flirting with the boys from school, some of them already starting work in the mines.

She loved to fetch water from the village well for her mother. Half way down the wooded slope a huge, lone beech tree grew, bringing back memories. In the spaces between its exposed roots she and her friends had played houses, the space between two roots becoming their "home". In the long, endless summer days they busied themselves playing shops as well. Sometimes they made little fire-grates of stones and cooked any vegetables they could obtain, whether given or stolen from their gardens, boiled in tins found in the rubbish holes. Gladys, Lily, Ivy and Dolly, where were they now? All capped and aproned in service in Cheltenham. The sight of this past play-centre brought on a wave of nostalgia that nearly turned to tears. On she went, down to the grassy steep bank where she had once found a single harebell growing, its daintiness quivering on its thin stem, enchanting her by its rareness in a habitat rich in the gaudy beauties of foxgloves and bluebells in their seasons. At the base of a steep bank and across a road, where the sight of a car was an exciting experience, the village men had built a wall round a natural spring. The stream from its overflow was full of frogs and tadpoles, and watercress. She picked a pocketful to take home, and drank several hand-cups of the lovely spring water.

A couple of times she walked into the little mining town two miles away whilst the children were at school and bought a bag of little fancy cakes for their tea, and often went out to play with them afterwards. Aldgate seemed a world away, but all too soon her two weeks had gone.

Back in Aldgate, without her services there was a general air of drabness. The kitchen range lacked polish, all the silver was tarnished and the front door knocker was dull, but there was an air of great excitement for Leah was soon to be married. The talk was of little else.

Laura wished it were Adam the son who was getting married. Despite the fact he was seriously engaged to a young Jewess, he tried to grab and kiss Laura if ever a chance occurred. She did not like Adam and found his habit of rubbing bread into greasy crumbs somehow repulsive. Although she found Adam's sly advances repugnant, she did not regard them seriously and knew if she told Momma it would mean the sack for her. Though the job had drawbacks, she did not relish going into another strange household. The Cohens were not snobs, except on the religious front, and she had grown fond of Rachel and had some affection for Momma. Anyway, Adam would no doubt marry when the finances of both sides were considered sufficient.

Leah was full of her wedding plans. She had a very good dress taste and big ideas. Sometimes David, who would be paying all the bills, gently remonstrated with her. She was going to live in a flat in Golders Green and the family were clubbing together to have a beautiful dining room suite made by a business acquaintance: everything was bought wholesale. The finest hall in the East End was booked, Leah's outfit decided on and the dresses for the bridesmaids chosen. The wedding feast would be in the early afternoon with the upstairs room booked for dancing and a social evening till midnight. Laura was invited too, with the duty of looking after four young children at a separate table. She was to be taken to the hall in a small cart with the driver who was taking a load of fancy cakes to eat when the four hours had elapsed after the wedding feast, for milk and meat eating must be separated by four hours.

The problem for Laura was, what to wear? But Lily, the oldest married daughter came to her aid. She would take Laura down Petticoat Lane and bargain for an outfit for her. It meant Laura had to sub two weeks' wages. Lily chose a pale peach silk dress, a wide brimmed cream straw hat with peach ribbon and a rose for trimming. Then, a novelty to Laura, some silk stockings and pair of high-heeled cream shoes, a pair of cream gloves to hide her swollen hands, and then her first lipstick and face-powder compact. Laura felt like Cinderella going to the ball.

When all the family had gone Laura got herself ready whilst waiting for the horse and trap to come with the cakes. After she had changed, put on some powder and lipstick and topped her freshly shampooed hair with the hat, she could not believe it was herself looking back at her from the full-length mirror in the bedroom. When the driver of the cart saw her, he whistled. "My word, you're a sight for sore eyes. I reckon you'll outdo the bride today!"

Laura was very impressed when she entered the hall. The banisters of the staircase were decorated with real flowers, while on the reception desk stood a huge glass bowl of punch with a silver ladle and glasses. Half the hall was the dining area and around the tables were seated about a hundred and fifty guests. If Laura was impressed with the grandeur of the hall, the diners who faced her were dumbstruck with admiration for her. Surely this beautiful creature couldn't be the Cohens' shiksa! Adam was overawed. Despite seeing her everyday, his carnal desires about her came to the boil, although his fiancée was sitting next to him. He thought, "What a fool I am, having such a tempting dish living in the same house, and not having a taste!"

David reacted too. He had already fallen in love with her, but knowing it was out of the question, he upbraided himself. His feelings were to protect and cherish her, and therefore leave her alone and banish romantic thoughts of her. But the vision she made today made him realise she had spoilt his desire for any other woman. He knew her to be intelligent and gentle and hardworking, a treasure of a young woman: a bargain indeed. Laura was not ambitious; she knew it was her lot to go into service from birth. There simply were no opportunities for much ambition for the very poor. Servants usually married men in unskilled or poorly paid jobs. They had no chance to meet the middle classes, except as their employers or the family of their employers. They in turn produced more children to do the unskilled, poorly paid jobs.

CHAPTER
FOUR

A couple of weeks after the wedding, Dolly's mistress called in. She was very worried about Dolly and feared she might lose her. The girl did nothing but cry and would not eat properly since her young man had dumped her for her friend. Please would Momma spare Laura for a couple of hours to keep Dolly company and maybe cheer her up? After much discussion and exclaiming, Momma finally agreed and Laura was pleased to get a chance to go out. Dolly had a very nice kitchen at the Levys' house. She was tear-stained and forlorn but put the kettle on for a cup of tea and some cake for Laura. "Bloody men!" moaned Dolly as she put the tea in front of Laura.

"What happened?" Laura asked.

"What happened? He ditched me for my so-called "friend". I'll expect she'll oblige him where I wouldn't. Men are only after one thing! I learnt my lesson about that with a bloke I used to go out with. He seemed a nice chap, didn't take too many liberties, if you know what I mean."

Laura did not.

"I met his mother and on my half-day off I used to go there to tea before we went to the pictures. Then one day his mother wasn't there; she'd gone to see her sister who was ill. We had the house to ourselves." Dolly continued, "'Course he persuaded me to go to bed with him. He said he'd be very careful and I'd be all right. To be truthful I didn't take all that much persuading. After that we were at it whenever we had the chance and a bit of privacy. Then one month I missed me period, then another, and I felt sick. His mother had cottoned on to what we were up to. I burst out crying and told her how I was. She was real mad, turned on her son and said if he was going to be a bloody fool, why didn't he make sure he went to the chemist first? Of course him and me had no money — we couldn't get married, but his mother said she knew a woman who would put me right for a couple of pounds. Well, I went — his mother made him pay. I felt awful, it was so embarrassing, but I didn't have that much pain. I finished with him after that and I made sure I wouldn't be a fool again until I had a wedding ring on my finger." Dolly sighed, "Now Dan, this bloke I've been going out with after that, wanted me to have sex with him. He kept on and on, but I stuck by my guns — so he ditched me for a rotten friend, and no doubts she'll be fool enough to give in to him. It's bloody miserable being on your own though. Why don't you demand your half-day off a week? It's the law, and we could go out together. In the summer instead of going to the pictures we could have our tea in a Lyons tea shop, then go window-shopping and sit in the park."

Backed by Mrs Levy, Momma had no grounds on which to object to Laura taking her weekly half-day off, and Laura loved to have a friend and confidant. Dolly was an attractive girl and Laura was a head-turner, so they got plenty of attention from men if they went in the park. They kept such meetings to mild flirtations, and fell in love with the screen heroes instead. It may be hard to believe, but Laura had no love life or the opportunity to meet the opposite sex. She only went out on errands to nearby shops, or otherwise as company for Rachel. She was so brainwashed by her humble beginnings and poverty that it did not occur to her to insist on time off on her own. Also, she did not talk to strangers, like so many working class girls who were very naïve and fearful until they were in their twenties.

To Laura's annoyance, Adam continued to pester her if the chance occurred, such as passing on the stairway. Laura, now eighteen was also a constant object of his brother's illicit, though honourable thoughts of her, which David could hardly control. When Leah married, Rachel went upstairs to sleep and Laura had the basement room to herself. She missed Rachel but was so tired out by bedtime, she was glad to get to sleep. Rachel still loved Laura's company, but she was an astute youngster and was aware that Adam and David admired Laura more that they should. She would not have approved had Laura responded, for Rachel was very Jewish in her beliefs, well grounded in her by her elderly, very orthodox, father.

Poppa grew weaker daily. Laura was cleaning vegetables in the scullery one late morning when she heard Momma cry out and hurry upstairs, screaming, "David! David, come quick! Poppa's choking!" Laura looked in the kitchen and Poppa sat on a chair by the range with his head back and with a rattling noise coming from his throat.

By the time David had rushed downstairs, he was gone. Laura stood there shocked, and when she saw David's face go grey and shrunken with grief and shock, she thought he was going too. "Oh Pop!" he groaned, and the agony in his eyes was unbearable. Then David took his mother in his arms and Laura went back into the scullery. The tears that were running down her cheeks were more for love and sympathy for David than for his poor dead father.

The whole family came down from the workshop and the grieving began. When Poppa's body had been taken, the family sat together in the room that was never used, weeping and wailing for many days, hardly eating except what Laura prepared with endless cups of tea. But life had to go on and eventually they went back to work upstairs. Momma took up her cooking again, Rachel's swollen, tear-stained eyes went back to normal and David, as the new head of the house, sat in Poppa's armchair by the range and took his place at head of the dining table. In time they practised a little freedom from Poppa's religious standards. They switched the lights on for themselves at Shabbat and did not go to the synagogue so much. But Laura still washed up the meat dishes in the scullery and the milk dishes in the kitchen.

Probably influenced by his desire for an agnostic girl, David began to doubt his religion. There were things in the Bible he could not accept, like Moses parting the Red Sea. If there was one untruth there could be others, and besides, wherever human beings lived they found something to worship, a need for some omnipotent power to give their own existence meaning. Such desires had spurred a lot of gods to which the human egos attached themselves, hating all the other religions who tried to cast doubt on their own particular deity and beliefs. Then it bred hatred and separation, which often led to war and murder. Because he was a Jew why should he not love a non-Jew? There was only the wall of religion to stop him. His mother noted he was worried and, putting it down to his single life, added to his stress by nagging him it was time to take a wife. Adam, on the other hand, had no problems of that sort. He was a Jew, glad to be a Jew, but felt that did not stop him going to bed with a Gentile if he had the choice. He continuously lusted after Laura, while her coolness and dislike of him made her more desirable.

CHAPTER
FIVE

Spring came, and with it a determination by Momma to rid the house of the patina of dirt left by the awful fogs on all the paintwork throughout the house, and there was an awful lot of paintwork! All the cleaning had to be finished by Passover. It meant carrying a set of steps around to reach the top of the windowpanes and the picture rails, on top of Laura's ordinary busy schedule. By bedtime Laura was utterly exhausted but Momma was in high good humour with her and bought her a very pretty sleeveless pink blouse. One half-day off, she had put it on and was making Momma and one of her friends a cup of lemon tea whilst she was waiting for Dolly, when she heard the friend say to Momma what sounded like, "Vos a tira shana maidel!" when looking at her. She asked Rachel what the words meant.

"A *very* pretty girl" Rachel told her. Laura had begun to realise she attracted attention, but apart from feeling pleased with herself, she had no notion of using her charms. For her, getting into bed to go to sleep as her head touched the pillow was what she looked forward to, the ring of her alarm clock at 6am coming much too soon.

It was about one o'clock in the morning after spring-cleaning when she struggled to consciousness with a feeling of a heavy weight on her and something choking her. Then the truth began to dawn on her that her body was being invaded by Adam who she so disliked. She struggled and tried to cry out, but he kept his hand over her mouth, urging her to "shush, shush, it's all right, it's only me, Adam . . ." and as she struggled for release he got his, and immediately regretted his actions. He rolled off her and sat on the side of the bed.

"How could you?" she moaned, "What about your girl friend? You are a pig and I hate you!"

He had treated her like men treated the bad girl Flossie in the village who everyone held in contempt.

"I'm sorry," he said quietly. "I promise never to touch you again. Don't tell anyone, please." and with that, shy and quiet as a cat, he crept up to his own room.

40

Laura could not think of sleeping. She wanted to plunge into a fast flowing river to wash herself clean. As she tossed restlessly in bed, thinking how she needed to wash away Adam's filth and her own disgrace, the loss of her innocence, her outrage at her violation and her fear for the future, the tears fell. Perhaps she would even let the river wash her away for ever? But she still felt unclean when the morning broke.

At breakfast Momma noticed how red and swollen Laura's eyes were, "Vot's the matter — vy you been cryin'?" she asked.

"I had a terrible nightmare. It upset me and I couldn't get back to sleep," was the answer.

"Nightmares? Young girls like you shouldn't be getting nightmares. Go now and get the rolls and coffee — maybe the fresh air vil make you feel better." It did not make Laura feel better, nothing made her feel better. She felt crushed, dirty and betrayed by life. She rushed to use the local baths, but she still felt unclean and too shocked to cope, so she kept quiet. Now she felt more like a robot than a lively girl with all her future to dream about. There was no one to share her terrible secret with, but true to his word, Adam had stopped pestering her. She wanted to leave the house immediately, but where could she go? She could not bear anyone to know this dreadful secret. Every night afterwards she locked her bedroom door.

CHAPTER
SIX

A couple of months later she was still very unhappy. "What's got into you?" Dolly demanded. "Anybody would think you got all the worries of the world on your shoulders."

"I feel I have!" moaned Laura, and burst out crying in the street.

"Something wrong at home?" Laura shook her head, too choked to speak. "Come on, tell me. It can't be all that bad."

"Oh it is" cried Laura. "I think I'm going to have a baby!"

Dolly replied, "You're mad! You've never had a fella, you soppy h'ap'th!"

"But I have," Laura replied, "I didn't want him, it was terrible and I feel so ashamed." Then the whole incident was poured into Dolly's amazed ears.

"The sod! The rotten sod! Why didn't you tell me before? You'll have to get rid of it. Maybe in the beginning you could have took some

Beecham pills and gin, that might have done it. Now you'll have to go to that woman I went to. My God, if Mr. David knew, he'd kill that Adam. Mr. David is a real gentleman — when he knew my mother had a serious operation he gave Mrs Levy the money for me to buy my Mum some Wincarnis wine. I'll tell you what, the Levys are gone out so we'll go back there and think what to do for the best." Dolly guided poor Laura by the arm.

By the time they were back in the Levys' kitchen, Dolly had formulated her plans. "Look, Laura, you'll have to get rid of it. It's not your fault it happened, you don't want a baby with that sod anyway, and think what a burden you would be to your mam and dad. But that woman charges — have you got any money?"

"Only my wages and thruppence," was the sad reply.

"Well, it's that Adam what will have to pay." Dolly took charge, "Now look, Laura, I'll write a note for you to give him, telling him what he's done to you, and that you will be able to get rid of it for five pounds by a woman you've heard of. She don't charge as much as that, but sting the bugger's pocket. Give him the note the first chance you've got. This evening before we go to the pictures. I'll take you round to see the woman and see if she'll get you out of your trouble next week. The quicker it's done the better. You will feel a bit rotten after and you bleed heavy, but you can tell Momma it's your period playing up. Do you agree it is the best you can do?"

"Yes, I suppose so," Laura was resigned. "I just feel I want to be as before that Adam touched me, but I can't and I do feel awful to think a strange woman can do this for me. I'm so embarrassed, Dolly!"

"I know how you feel, Laura," she replied, "I've been through it, but it was worse for me because it had been partly my fault. Now just you copy this note out and mind and give it him, then we'll go and see if that woman's in."

Glad to have shared her burden with her friend Laura whispered. "Thanks Dolly" and gave her a hug before sitting down to copy the note.

The woman lived in a terrace of small houses divided into an upstairs and a basement flat; she lived in the basement. She answered the door but peered up and down the street to see if anyone else was about before she asked them in. She recognised Dolly and wanted to know if anyone else knew about this visit. Dolly assured her not , and explained why she had brought Laura, which the woman had already surmised. Two monthly periods missed and another week to wait. Yes, she was sure she could put Laura out of her trouble and the charge would be three pounds and the transaction to be absolutely confidential. Laura was only too glad to agree with this. The woman abortionist looked a pleasant motherly figure, but there was an odour about her, which Laura had mentioned to Dolly. Dolly had noticed it too and recognised it as gin. "Cheer up now", said Dolly, "By this time next week it will be all over, and if I was you I'd leave the Cohens and get another job," she advised.

It was a couple of days before Laura managed to slip the note to Adam, for he was indeed keeping his word to leave her alone. She got a five-pound note in an envelope the following day from a worried looking Adam. On the girls' next free half day, they made their way to the dismal basement, looking round about as she had instructed to make sure that nobody was watching them. The gin on the woman's breath was stronger than before, but she was pleasant and friendly. Laura tried mentally to disassociate herself from what was happening to her, but was flushed and humiliated when it was time to dress herself. The procedure had been painful, she was bleeding a little but was well protected by the sanitary pads she been told to bring. She paid the three pounds and still had two pounds left to treat Dolly to the pictures and send some money home to her mother. The relief was inexpressible. Dolly gave her a hug and they started on their way to the cinema.

CHAPTER
SEVEN

After just a few steps, suddenly Laura gave a cry of pain and doubled up, unable to walk. Blood began to pour down her leg, but by the greatest of luck a philanthropic taxi driver spotted them, and he drew up. "'Op in, I'll take you to the 'orspital!" He kindly waived any payment and a terrified Dolly handed Laura over to a couple of nurses.

Later, removing his bloody gown and washing his hands outside the operating theatre, the weary surgeon turned to the ward staff nurse who had come to collect Laura after surgery. "Any sign of the repentant boyfriend, Nurse?" he asked.

"Oh no, sir, I don't think there was a boyfriend involved," she replied, "The friend who brought her to Casualty said she had been raped."

"Oh, not another of these kitchen drudges ignorant of the facts of life and too frightened to ward off the master!" He had heard it all before.

"Probably! Was a hysterectomy necessary?" the nurse asked.

"Fortunately not this time. I could only find a single perforation of the uterus which I managed to darn, but I want observations every 15 minutes all night for signs of haemorrhage."

"She was one of the lucky ones then?" The nurse had seen too many young girls admitted after these illegal abortions, and thought it a hard judgement to be made infertile at the age of nineteen.

"Well, she still has her womb, if that's what you mean. I'm keeping theatre on alert tonight since if the sutures can't hold, we'll have to do an emergency hysterectomy."

The nurse adjusted the flow of the blood transfusion, and in answer to the doctor's enquiry said, "Yes, we have three more pints cross-matched."

As he took off his blood-splattered gown, he said, "In a way, the haemorrhage was partly beneficial since it probably rinsed away some bacteria, but there is the real danger of infection to come." The staff nurse helped the porter wheel Laura away to the ward, and the theatre sister sighed, "How are we ever going to stop these back street abortionists mutilating young innocent girls?"

"The poor girls never reveal their names and addresses so the police are helpless," the doctor answered, "And the guilty men just pay the abortionist's bill and then continue their attentions to the next maid who comes to the house."

"Well, we only see those who are brought alive to the hospital — only last month there were three in our district who died of haemorrhage before they got here." The theatre sister shared his feeling of despair.

When Laura was conscious again after the anaesthetic, the surgeon came to her bedside and the ward sister pulled the curtains round her bed, enclosing them for some semblance of privacy. Laura was still dazed and bewildered by the rapid turn of events. She remembered walking with Dolly with a feeling of relief that the very unpleasant previous event was now just an episode she could put behind her, then the sudden pain, leaning on Dolly and being helped out of a car by someone in a uniform, but very little else. Now she woke up in a clean hospital bed with blood dripping into her arm, feeling alarmed but dozy.

"Are you well enough to tell me what happened?" the surgeon kindly asked. Laura kept her mouth shut tightly and turned away her head in shame on her pillow.

"Well, if it was an illegal abortion, we will have to make a police report." When he noticed Laura's distress he added, "But that can wait till later." Laura did not want to think about it. There was a lot she did not want to think about just now: meeting Adam again, giving in her notice and finding a new job, her parents, her future . . .

The surgeon continued, "You are a very lucky girl. The cab driver saved your life, you know, since you were bleeding dangerously." Laura tried to say something, but the surgeon patted her hand and added, "If everything goes well, we hope you will recover fully and be able to have children later, but it is too early to tell now. Rest and time will heal. You will feel stronger when we have replaced the blood you lost, and I'll talk to you again in a few days," and with that he left.

Laura had not said a word, but once she had been left alone the tears fell silently down her cheeks, wetting the pillow. They were caused by a mixture of so many feelings she could not really separate; relief, shame, self-pity, gratitude, exhaustion, bewilderment, loneliness, pain, and also some sorrow for the new little life she had taken. But after the nurse gave her an injection for the pain, she fell asleep and her worries were over for that day.

Meanwhile Dolly had been waiting impatiently for news of her friend. It seemed a lifetime before a young doctor came into the waiting room. "Are you the person with the young woman who was haemorrhaging?" She nodded. "Well, first I must tell you she's lucky to be alive. She's been to an abortionist, hasn't she?" he asked, knowing the answer. Dolly nodded. "A woman in a back street, I've no doubt. Do you know who was responsible for the girl's condition?"

"Yes, sir," Dolly answered, "It was the son of the people she works for, she's their maid. He forced himself on her in the night — it wasn't her fault — she doesn't even like him. And he's already engaged to someone."

"Well, we shall have to keep her in for a while; she's lost a lot of blood. I'll give you a letter for her employers — see that they get it, will you?"

"Yes, sir — can I see her please?" Dolly asked.

"No, not just yet. If you can wait, I'll tell a nurse to let you know when she's come round fully from the anaesthetic."

Later, when she was allowed to see her, Dolly wept as she saw how ill Laura looked, "Oh I'm so sorry, Laura!" she cried.

Laura murmured weakly, "Don't be, at least it's over now."

"The doctor has given me a letter about you to give to your employers, but Momma can't read and she will go mad if she knows the truth. I'll give it to Mr. David. I reckon it would be better if he told the family you've had your appendix out. What do you think?" Dolly asked.

"Oh yes, that's a good idea." Laura added wearily, "Anyway I shall give my month's notice in when I'm out of the hospital."

Dolly looked at the hospital clock for the time. She knew it was a habit of Mr. David's to work on in his office after the others had left and she hurried there. She decided to pull the door key on the string and let herself in and hoped he was still upstairs. Luck was with her. He looked very surprised to see her and with such a tear-stained face.

"What's the matter, Dolly, is there something wrong?" he asked. She handed him the letter. He read it eagerly, then his face went grey before becoming suffused deep red with shock and fury.

Looking up at her, he asked, "Is this true, Dolly?"

"Yes, Mr. David," she replied, "But it wasn't Laura's fault. She woke up to find him in her bed! She doesn't like Adam; she's often said how different you are for brothers. She thinks you're a proper gentleman." Dolly added.

Her comment was a glimmer of light in this black disgraceful scenario. He began to pace up and down the office. "I could kill my brother! I don't blame Laura at all. I just feel shattered this has been done to her in this house. Momma must never know, Dolly, it would kill her!"

"We thought of that," she said, "You could say it was a burst appendix."

"Oh my God, that swine of a brother! To do this to a lovely girl like Laura! I'll make him pay where it hurts!" David cried. "Not that he can ever make up to her for what he has done." He added, "Please, Dolly, keep the truth to yourself. For Laura's sake and Momma's."

"Yes, Mr. David, I will, for I feel guilty that I took her to that woman who did it, though she meant well."

David asked, "Dolly, what did it cost?"

"I made her ask Adam for the money because it would have taken too long for her to save it up — it was five pounds." she replied.

"I'll pay Laura a lot more than that before I've finished with her, and here's something for you, Dolly." and he pulled a pound note from his pocket.

"Oh thank you, Mr. David, but I don't want anything." and she blushed for his error. As he stood there, Rachel came up with a message from Momma — When was David coming for his meal? "And why," she asked, "was Dolly coming down the stairs?"

"It's Laura," he replied, "She was taken ill when she and Dolly were out. Dolly took her to hospital with a burst appendix," he explained. "I'm just off to see her."

Rachel asked, "Can I come, David?"

"Not this time, Pet," and he ruffled his sister's hair.

"In hospital? How come?" Momma shrieked. "'Ow can I manage if she's in hospital?"

"Well you'll just have to get a cleaning woman like you had before Laura came." David answered, "I'm just off to see how she is."

"But your meal is waiting, and ze others have eaten already." Momma remonstrated.

"Put it on the hob to keep warm." he suggested, and he was gone.

His mind was in turmoil. He did not feel his own slate was quite clean. He knew he too desired Laura but it was with his mind and heart as well as his loins. He would only take her to bed with his wedding ring on her finger. His anger at Adam's betrayal made him feel physically ill. What a problem his love for Laura was. He thought of his two older sisters. Like Leah, they had been introduced to their partners by the marriage broker and seemed happy enough, but he would be a cheat. He knew he had already lost his right to an arranged marriage by letting Laura take his heart, and she did not even know. His feelings intensified when he was shown into the cubicle where Laura lay looking pale and sleepy and almost ethereal. One of her arms was bandaged and a rubber tube leading from a glass bottle slowly dripped blood into her vein. Her other arm was out on the coverlet. He sat down on the chair by the side of the bed and picked up her work-swollen hand and kissed it.

"Oh Laura, I'm so sorry this terrible thing has happened to you. I could kill my brother for what he has done. I know that you are in no way to blame. Oh Laura, it would destroy my mother if she knew and I'm glad my father never lived to know. I am lying to the family, Laura, telling them you have a burst appendix. When you are better, I will take you home to your parents and explain how you were betrayed under my roof, and I will make Adam pay dearly for his behaviour. Laura, my dear, will you let me deceive the family for my mother's sake?" he asked.

Laura could only answer, "Of course, Mr. David."

"Laura, I can understand my brother desiring you but I cannot believe his stupidity." And then he had to say it, "Laura, I love you myself." Laura could hardly believe what she was hearing, "But I love you for your character as much as for your beauty. To me you are a superior young lady, too good to be a household drudge for the likes of us. I know any hopes for me where you are concerned are just foolish dreaming." He looked at her face, "Are you in pain, my dear?"

Utterly bewildered, but not angry with David's confession, for she realised she could love him too, she said, "No, I'm feeling a bit weak but the pain has gone. It feels strange to be doing nothing and being waited on." Just then a doctor came in and David stood up to go.

"Just a minute." the doctor said, "Would you step outside for a moment"? He closed the door so the patient could not hear them, and asked, "Can you tell me what is your relationship with this young lady?"

"I'm her employer."

"Are you responsible for her recent condition?" he asked.

"No! Most certainly not! But I do know who is and that Miss Bailey is a completely blameless victim. I intend to punish the culprit and make sure he pays for a long convalescence. I shall take her home to the country to her parents. She is our maid, you see."

"Yes, I gathered she was a domestic worker by her hands." (David winced.) "She should be well enough to be discharged in a few days. Her unwelcome pregnancy has ended but God knows what scars it has left on her mind."

David went back to kiss the top of Laura's head and promised he would bring Rachel to see her on the morrow.

"That's another admirer of yours, I see," smiled the doctor, who, if the truth be told, was a bit smitten himself, for Laura was a very beautiful girl.

The next day, with a bunch of flowers, some fruit and some of Momma's chicken soup, David and Rachel went to visit Laura.

"Will you come back to us when you're better?" Rachel wanted to know. "Momma's lost without you. We've got our old cleaner back, but she's ancient and can't do a quarter of the work you did." Laura let Rachel chatter on without answering. She was sure she wouldn't go back to the Cohens but she now realised she loved David and would be sorry never to see him again.

When Dolly had her half-day off, she made straight for the hospital. "Oh Laura, what a fright you gave me! I was scared you were going to die! I've never seen anybody as angry as Mr. David when I told him what had happened. Mind you, I reckon he fancies you himself, but he knows it could never come to anything as he has to marry a Jewess, but he's too much of a gentleman to show it."

"Gosh, Dolly, I reckon you're a witch! He told me he loved me when he came the first time," Laura confided in her friend. "He hasn't said anything since, but he comes to visit every evening, sometimes with Rachel."

"And do you love him, Laura?"

Laura thought for a while, then the realisation came to her, and she answered simply, "I think I do, Dolly."

When David arrived home on the first evening he had gone to the hospital, he could hardly swallow any of his evening meal. He was full of anger and worry. Adam had gone out, unaware of what had happened. David decided to wait up in Adam's bedroom till he came home. When, very late, the door opened and Adam came in, David closed the door and gave Adam a slap across the face that sent him reeling on to the bed. "What's that for?" he demanded.

"You pig! You disgrace to the family! You know what that's for! You raped Laura a couple of months ago — she's in hospital, having nearly lost her life going to a back street abortionist to get rid of your sins. I could kill you for such selfish madness. But I'll make sure she will have a very long convalescence at your expense."

Adam answered, "I'm sorry. I'm truly ashamed. I let the sight of her about the house play on my mind. My God, do Momma and the others know?"

"No, for Laura and their sake I've told them a lie — they think she was rushed to hospital with appendicitis when she was out with Dolly. Dolly, bless her, isn't going to give you away, but she hates the sight of you."

At the hospital Dolly said, "You never told me you fancied David, Laura."

"Well, I never thought of him in that way," she explained, "But he's such a nice man, Dolly, and so good to his family. I do admire him but I never dreamt he had any feelings for me. I know he can never marry a Gentile, but I can't help it, I think I do love him."

"Well anyway, Laura, it would never work. Momma would throw a fit if she had any idea of what two of her sons were thinking, and the rest of the family would be dead against such an idea. Marrying Out indeed!"

"He said he wanted me more than anything in the world, but only with his marriage ring on my finger."

"Did he say you would have to become a Jew?" Dolly asked, perplexed.

"No, he knows I wouldn't. I couldn't, Dolly, ever be such a hypocrite. Anyway, I think he's too clever to be really religious himself."

"What a pickle you've got yourself in 'cos you're so pretty, Laura. It's just like something on the films. When you get home are you going to tell your dad and mam what happened?" she asked.

Laura explained, "David is going to take me home, he said it's his duty to tell them the truth and that it was not my fault."

"He's brave, then! Do you think your dad might wallop him one?" Dolly enquired.

Laura thought, "No! My dad's not that sort, but he'll be very upset and if he met Adam he might hit him."

"Do you know when you'll be discharged?"

"Next Thursday, they said." replied Laura.

"I shall miss you Laura." said Dolly sadly. "We'll keep in touch. Maybe you'll get another job where we can go out together on our half-days? I've got a piece of paper and a pencil in my bag so I'll write down your home address. I *do* want us to stay friends."

"Me too!" Laura agreed.

When the nurses had brought tea and a cup for Dolly, Laura persuaded her not to miss the picture and promised to write to Dolly when she got home. Rachel came to fetch Laura from hospital the following Thursday. Without too much demur from Momma, Laura insisted on cleaning all the silver and the copper samovar ready for Shabbat before going home the following day. It was to the surprise of the family apart from Adam that David insisted on taking Laura home to the country himself.

CHAPTER
EIGHT

Laura got her first ride in a taxi on the way to Paddington Station. They spoke very little on the journey but now and again David would put his hand over hers, and a feeling of warmth and contentment overcame Laura. When the train stopped at the little halt about a mile from her village, David was as much amazed at the terrain as Laura been when first seeing London. The main road was about a quarter of a mile away and as far as the eye could see empty, for a car in those days would have been a great novelty there. Laura showed him the village well, built round a spring by the road, then they crossed to a pathway through a forest of oak trees with undergrowth of ferns and foxgloves. "What beauty!" David marvelled, and what a contrast this nature's palace was to the humble stone dwellings of the village. At her parents' house, they passed through the garden gate made from an old iron bedstead, up the path and in through the front door to where Laura's parents sat shyly in their tidy best clothes. Laura noticed the best rag-made rug from upstairs was now in front of the downstairs fireplace and the best treasured cups and saucers, got from saving tea packet coupons, were on the table. The first awkward moments were helped by Laura's mother bustling about, making tea from the big black kettle boiling on the hob of an old-fashioned grate.

"What a beautiful area you live in!" observed David.

"I agree with you," replied her dad, "but it's got its ugly areas, thanks to the interference of man."

"How do you mean?"

"The pit areas and the squalid conditions the Foresters have to live under," he explained. David realised at once this was no ordinary working man, this was where Laura's intelligence came from.

"I suppose we wouldn't appreciate beauty if there was no ugliness," David replied.

"Yes, everything must have its opposites, but we ought to try to get a better balance in the world on the lovely side." Laura's father responded.

"Never mind about those things," interjected her mother, "Drink this tea whilst it's hot and please try a bit of my home-made cake."

"Now what has our Laura had the matter, and is she all right now?" and she put her arm around her daughter and kissed her as she spoke.

"That's why I have brought her home." David replied, "Her father just said how much better the world would be if man controlled his ugly instincts more, and how I agree with him. It is very hard for me to have to tell you this, but your beautiful daughter has known the ugly side of man through no fault whatever of her own, except to be born beautiful. I have nothing but praise and admiration for her. She was a wonderful help to my mother, hard-working, cheerful and a great companion for my twelve-year old sister. Laura's intelligence impressed us all. She is much too superior to have to get her living as a domestic servant." Laura's parents smiled at each other.

David continued, "Alas and I'm mortified to have to say it, my younger brother Adam went down to Laura's bedroom in the early hours and raped a defenceless, sleeping, overworked girl." Laura' parents were horrified. David continued, "She struggled but it was too late. She cried for days but wouldn't tell us what had upset her, then two months later our neighbour's servant girl who had become friendly with Laura took her to a back street abortionist to risk her life, getting rid of my brother's sin." Laura's mother gasped and clapped her hand to her mouth. "She didn't want to be a burden to you. Fortunately, she quickly got to a hospital that tried to repair the damage and replace some of the lost blood. But Laura is still weak and needs looking after." He added vehemently, "I hate my brother, I think sometimes I could kill him for what he's done."

Laura started to cry. Her father took her on his arm, "There, there, my wench. We know you would never 'ave done anything to let your old Mam and Dad down."

"I'm sorry, sir." David said, touching her father's shoulder, and the tears were in his eyes, too.

"Sorry, Dad," said Laura, and they all sat down again.

"I must get back to London." David said. "I know too well nothing I can do will make up for what has happened to Laura under my roof, but my brother will only get pocket money wages for the next couple of years — and this will ensure

Laura can have a long convalescence," and he put an envelope on the table.

Laura went with him to the garden gate. "I love you, Laura, I can't help it," David confessed, "I know it's hopeless, but please let me know if I can ever be a help to you." He kissed her hand, and with tears misting her eyes, she watched him disappear down the woodland path.

Her parents were still sitting, shocked at what they had heard. "Do you feel all right now?" they asked. "We would never have let you go to London if we'd known this would happen," Her father added.

"I must say his brother might be a bad sort, but he's a proper gentleman. Did you hear him call your father "sir"? And you better open the envelope to see what he's left you." her mam said.

"It's for you, Mam, to keep me till I find another job. I'll look for one soon."

"Look for one soon?" her mother exclaimed, "There'll be no need of that. Just look what he's left! A fortune of two hundred pounds! You shall have some smart new clothes and get a job in a shop or something different to domestic service."

When the Bailey family paid off all their bills and started spending money, it was soon around the village that Laura had been in hospital and her employer had brought her home. The family said she had suffered a burst appendix, but some wily individuals guessed that was a new name for a bastard. Probably the boss had got her pregnant and paid to get rid of it. She *was* an uncommonly pretty girl! Whatever, she became a minor celebrity in the village for a while.

There was another celebrity in the village: a young man called Aden Johansson who was uncannily gifted at football and worked in the coal mine.

CHAPTER
NINE

Back at Leman Street, Momma often bewailed the loss of Laura. Rachel missed her badly too, but with a sense of relief. She had become aware of David's fondness for Laura and her Jewish instincts resisted any thought of a serious relationship. Momma also bewailed David's lax attitude towards matrimony. It fell on deaf ears. David was bewitched by his hopeless longing for Laura, but apart from a letter from her and her parents thanking him gratefully for his generosity, there had been no contact.

One day, tortured by his frustration, he decided to go and see Laura. It might put the dream to rest and he could get on with his life apart from business, which had progressed so well he was going to move the workshop to larger premises.

He did not tell his family where he was going. He got off the train at the forest halt, and as he walked through the woods to the village he leant against a tree and berated himself. What was he doing, a thirty-six year old Jew chasing a twenty-year old, penniless Gentile? He was crazy, his mind told him, but his heart answered that he would brave the scorn of his family, even sacrifice his place in their hearts, to have Laura for his wife. How would her parents view the idea after what had happened? He sighed deeply and walked on. Laura's two younger sisters were playing hopscotch on a flat piece of earth by the garden gate.

"Hallo!" he called, "Are your parents and Laura indoors?"

"No, only Mam and me brother. Dad's at work and Laura will be home soon 'cos it's early closing day in the shop where she works." A wave of joy went through him at the thought of seeing Laura again. Her brother Tim was indoors having a badly grazed knee bathed by his mother, who was giving him scolding and sympathy in equal measures for climbing up the tree to cause this injury. She was utterly astonished when she answered the tap on the door to see David.

"Why, Mr. Cohen! Do come in please." she smiled. "I'll put the kettle over the fire and get you a cup of tea."

"Forgive me for calling unexpectedly, but I had some business down this way," (the fibber) "and thought I'd call in to see how Laura was getting on," he explained.

"Oh she's fine, greatly thanks to you. She'll be home in a few minutes. She works in the town now in a dress shop, but it's half-day closing today." Her words went through David like nectar. He was going to see Laura! He was glad to sit down and wait since he was trembling with anticipation.

Then young Tim piped up, "Our Laura's going to be married, and look 'oo it's to. 'Ere's 'is photo in the paper — look!" and he held up a folded sheet of the local newspaper which showed a photograph of Aden Johansson, young and handsome with a physique to match, in the act of kicking a goal.

"He's the best footballer you ever saw, he's semi-professional, 'cos the pit manager lets 'im 'ave time off to play for G — — town, and they pay 'im," Tim said proudly. The words fell like lead on David's spirits. Laura was going to be married! No, no, it couldn't be! "You fool!" he thought, "Why not? A girl like Laura must have had loads of men tell her they love her. She's young and pretty and a woman with a woman's needs. She was grown-up now and why should she even give me a thought when there were chaps like that Johansson ready to marry her?" Now he must come to his senses. Perhaps when he saw her again the magic would have gone. For a minute he was too shocked to speak, then with a superhuman effort, he found a calm voice.

"Thank you for the tea. I'm sure Laura will be happy — she certainly deserves to be. I must be getting on to catch my train. Perhaps I shall meet Laura on the way." and he rose to go.

"Won't you stay and have a meal with Laura? She'll be sorry to have missed you. I'm sure she will be delighted and very surprised to see you," Mrs. Bailey urged.

"No, I won't stay. Please give my kindest regards to your husband," and he was off.

He hadn't gone very far through the woods before he saw her coming in his direction. The magic of her had not gone, but the hopes of ever having her had, and he found it hard to speak.

"Why, Mr. Cohen! What a surprise! Is everyone all right at Leman Street?" Laura was astonished to see him there.

"Yes, the family are all right. I want to feel happy about you getting married and if I was a gentleman I would be. But I'm not, Laura, I feel I could die of misery now. I can hold no hope of making you mine. Do you love this young man? Well, of course you do, but I was beginning to think you had feelings for me. No fool like an old fool, I suppose!" was his outburst.

"Oh but I do feel for you!" Laura declared. "I admire you and think you are a very good man. It's just I never thought of you except as my mistress's son. I never dreamt you would look at someone like me to be serious about," she explained.

"I shouldn't do, Laura, but it's as impossible to stop me wanting you as to stop the water flowing down Niagara Falls. But now you yourself have made it out of the question. I have to accept that. But Laura, as long as I live, whatever turns my life takes, I shall always be your friend if you need me." He kissed her warmly on the cheek and she returned the compliment with a kiss on his.

When he had gone, she leant against the tree, her heart pounding with agitation. She knew if she could turn the clock back, she would not have encouraged Aden to propose to her. She knew that it was David she loved and David whose need was greatest. Aden was a nice young man, fit, handsome and a local hero in all the masculine eyes. Life for him was uncomplicated days of contentment and she was just another string to his bow. There were plenty of other girls he could choose from, but she knew what David felt for her was on a much deeper level. It was too late now, and besides, David would be an outcast among his own family if he married her. And what would her parents think of her marrying her Jewish boss over a decade older than herself? She had made her choice and she must stick to it.

At home, her mother was full of chat about Mr. Cohen's brief visit and was glad he had been able to see her. "There's no doubt he regards you highly and is probably still worried about his brother's behaviour," her mam speculated on the reason for his visit. Normally hungry for her meal when she came home from work, that evening Laura had a job to eat anything.

CHAPTER
TEN

It was a very pretty wedding. The church was packed and every girl in the congregation day-dreamed that when she grew up, she would be like Laura Bailey and have a beautiful long white dress and marry someone like Aden Johansson. All the males, young and not so young, envied Aden.

They rented a small two-up, two-down cottage situated on its own a short distance from the village, for three and sixpence a week. It had its own well and a large garden. Laura knew how lucky she was and tried to be happy. She still went to work and managed the household chores, and did quite a lot of gardening. Only now and again did she stand and stare and not be able to stop herself thinking tenderly of David.

Back in Leman Street Momma sighed. She missed the work of Laura, but if the truth be told, also her company. She sighed over her

David, still holding out against the services of a marriage broker, getting more and more involved with the expanding business, and with more grey hairs showing at the temple. To David's great relief, Adam got married and went to work for his father-in-law.

It was normal practice when the factory upstairs had their elevenses for David to come downstairs to have his in the kitchen with his mother, and read the paper. A few months later he had turned to the sporting pages at the back, when a photograph caught his eye. It was the same one that Laura's brother had shown him of Aden Johansson. It went with the tragic headline, *Young Promising Footballer Killed in Pit Fall.* David stared in surprise and horror. What a terrible blow for Laura and all concerned! He could not help the thought that Laura was free again entering his mind, but he would not have wished it so in so cruel a fashion. His mother noticed his face.

"Something bad in the paper, son?"

"Yes, Momma, a terrible tragedy. A young fellow killed in a pit fall in a coal mine."

"Ach, such awful things to happen, and here's me grumbling for things I shouldn't. Poor boy, poor boy! Vot must his mother be feelink?"

David folded the paper and took it upstairs with him. He read it again in the office to let it sink in. Laura was a window. More than ever, he wanted to comfort her and marry her. It was too soon to intrude but he could send her a letter of condolence.

Like all the accidents at the mine, the tragedy hung over the village like a pall of poisonous fog. For a long time shoulders slouched, legs dragged, and laughter was muted, if it sounded at all. Pity for Laura was boundless. She stayed with her parents for the week of the funeral, then went back to her own cottage until she could sort out what to do. Perhaps she would write to Dolly and ask her to get her a job? She was like a ship adrift. In the end she agreed with her parents and decided to move back to her childhood home to help with her siblings and keep her local job while she decided what to do in future, but she did write to Dolly and tell her that she had become a widow.

Back in London, Dolly did not think there was any harm in repeating Laura's news to her mistress, and when Mrs. Levy met Momma Cohen at the market the following Thursday, she repeated what Dolly had told her.

"You want to hear a tragedy? Apparently your girl Laura went and got married back in the country. But it was a short affair: her husband went and got himself killed and left her penniless again."

"Ach, vot a tragedy. So young for a vidow already!" Mrs. Cohen exclaimed, wondering to herself if she could in time offer Laura her old job.

Laura grieved for Aden, for although she had not found her true mate type in him, it broke her heart to think he had died so young, and she grieved for his parents who had been so full of pride for him, and now had only memories to sustain them. She wrote back to David's consolation letter and he kept the letter in his breast pocket as it kept a feeling of hope in his heart. He began to feel hopeful. Everyone back home noticed the difference in his mood. They wondered and conjectured, had he found someone for a bride for himself? His sisters whispered the idea to Momma and she beamed at David and waited expectantly for good news from him

CHAPTER
ELEVEN

When a few months had passed and Momma still had not discovered if her son had found himself a sweetheart at last, David decided to go and see Laura again. He wrote to her parents to say he was coming, but asking that they keep his visit a secret. It would be a surprise for Laura when she saw him, and he would know by her reaction if he stood any chance.

After leaving the train, on his way through the woodland path to Laura's parents' home, David suddenly stopped, overwhelmed by the nature of his actions. What was he doing? He, a Jew in his late thirties, determined to marry a Gentile! Not merely a Gentile, but one over a decade younger than himself with no money, from a strangely different background and culture. By marrying her he would cause perhaps insurmountable problems with his own family.

He leant against a tree, his heart pounding with emotion and indecision. Then along the pathway came Laura, and the surge of love which enveloped him at the sight of her sent all doubts fleeing.

"Oh darling!" was all he could say when he took her in his arms. Then Laura knew that to be with David was all she wanted in life. Hand in hand, they set off together. When they had gone a few paces, he stopped. Putting a hand on her shoulder and tilting her face up to look him squarely in the eye, he asked, "Laura, do you want to be my wife as much as I with all my heart and soul want to be your husband?"

Her eyes were two luminous orbs of truth as she answered, "Yes, David." At last she felt really sure that they could make each other happy. But she added, "The only sadness is that your family will object."

"That's it, then! Nothing will stop me now!" and he hugged her with confidence running like honey through his veins.

Indoors, Laura's parents sat in a mood of nervous expectancy. They wore their Sunday best. The black iron grate shone with a kettle singing on the hob. The downstairs rag rugs had been replaced for the day with the less worn rugs from the bedrooms, and the stone flagged floor was scrubbed clean enough to eat off. Handshaking over and everyone seated, Mrs. Bailey bustled about making a pot of tea, and when the four of them had a cup, Laura's father spoke up.

"As you can imagine, young man, this has come as a great surprise to Laura's mother and me. In our experience all the women we know who have gone into domestic service have been treated as inferior human beings, although sadly occasionally not too inferior to rape. I would like to state now that I do not think you will be lowering yourself in any way if you married Laura." Mrs. Bailey nodded her agreement.

"To my mind she is good enough for any man in the world. Of course," continued Laura's father, "our main concern is for Laura's happiness. She's suffered too much for any young woman, through no fault of her own."

"Oh, I know that Mr. Bailey, and I want if I can, to redress the balance. I promise I will be as good a husband as possible. At the very least, I can provide her with a very comfortable standard of living." David assured them.

"Your actions bear out your words, young man, but marriage is a two-sided arrangement and we want to feel sure Laura feels the same way about you. I think I know my daughter well enough that she won't be unduly influenced by your money, but the difference it would make in her life could be an attraction that could prove hollow if her love for you doesn't match your love for her."

Then looking at Laura, he asked "Do you want to marry Mr. Cohen, my wench? And I want you to be sure before you answer. Remember, your new in-laws won't own you, I suppose, and you may be very lonely on your own. Well, you'll have your husband, of course. Think well before you answer."

"I have thought about it, Dad. When I worked for David's mother, I used to think what a nice man he was, so good to his family, so hard working. And when he talked and expressed opinions I thought he was nearly as clever as you, Dad. But I never gave him a thought as my young man. It was only when I was in hospital and he told me how much he thought of me that I realised I loved him too. Even when I married Aden, Dad, I felt guilty that I like David so much."

Mr. Bailey began to philosophise, "We are hidebound by caste systems and from what I have gathered the Jewish religion is very strong. The members think they are the chosen followers of God. A myth I think, which has caused some anti-Semitism from other religious groups. In this village we have a little primitive Methodist chapel so we are primitive Methodists. What you are in religion depends on where you are born."

"Very true," murmured Mrs. Bailey.

Laura's father continued, "Mankind is haunted by two questions, his origins and his mortality. He cannot understand the former and he cannot face up to the latter. From his tortured imagination in different parts of the world he has produced gods and devils to account for human behaviour. Worship the chosen god and follow his rules, and you will get everlasting life in a place called Heaven. Behave badly and deny him, and you will go to a place called Hell, where you would burn everlasting. This god was made in human form to satisfy man's ego and anything more absurd I cannot imagine. Just think — one god in human form as ruler of this complex planet with its millions of ever-growing, replenishing life forms! The thought defies any kind of logic and makes one wonder why the earth was once populated by prehistoric animals, as we have proof of by finding their remains."

Mr. Bailey looked David in the eyes, "Yet so strong are these man-made myths that you and Laura will be made outcasts by your family for rejecting their religious beliefs. No doubt to create a god and a devil was a smart move by some great minds in the past, to make human beings behave, but it hasn't worked: by creating too many gods they have created hate and doubts. Look at the tragedy of Ireland, for example."

"I follow your line of thought," David replied, "but it is a hard philosophy to follow that life, especially individual life, has no meaning. You cannot blame humanity for seeking some comfort and logic out of it. Although I'm a Jew I have read *The Origin of Species* by Charles Darwin and it sent me down your pathway of thinking."

"Well, I'm thinking it's time we had something to eat." said Laura's mam, and broke up the conversation by laying the table.

"A delicious meal, thank you very much", said David later, patting his stomach. "And now for the big question: will you give your blessing to our marriage?"

"If Laura wants to go ahead, I've certainly no objection. How about you, Mother?" Mr. Bailey asked his wife.

"With all my heart," she replied, "I'm only interested in Laura's happiness." The two men shook hands warmly and David got up and kissed Mrs Bailey on each cheek. "I'm pricelessly indebted to you both!" he laughed. Then he took a box from his pocket.

"You know us Jews! We always know someone in the trade. Well, I know a *good* jeweller and he's lent me these six engagement rings to see if Laura would chose one of them. I've already chosen one for myself if I'm lucky." All the rings were lovely and by luck fitted, as Laura's hands were no longer swollen with hard labour. Finally she settled on a half-hoop and he slipped it onto her finger with a kiss.

"Now we're engaged, darling, and I'm the happiest man in the world!" he said as he hugged her.

"And it's time for a glass of my homemade parsnip wine!" and Laura's mother got up to fetch the bottle and glasses.

Just then the children came in from their long walk home from school. David looked at his watch. "Good heavens! I must get going or I'll miss my train," and after hugs and kisses and a half crown each from David for Laura's brothers and sisters, he and Laura had to run most of the way through the woods to get to the little station halt with only a minute to spare. As the train to London pulled out and she waved goodbye to him, her heart was full of a happiness that she so recently had imagined impossible she could ever experience again.

CHAPTER
TWELVE

David could now make his plans. He would not rush Laura. When she was ready, he would arrange a registry office wedding in London and pay her parents' expenses to come up by train. Then they would all go to the West End for a meal. In the meantime he would set out to look for a house in Golders Green. When he found what he thought would be a suitable one, Laura could come and stay for a weekend in a local hotel and see if it suited her. Over the weekend she could come with him to choose carpets and furniture, then whenever it was ready they could move in to start married life,

As he took his seat in the train back, his mood deflated rather as he thought of telling the family his decision. They would all be shocked, especially his mother, and the thought pained him. He decided to get it over as soon as possible, so told all the family to be at Leman Street the next Friday evening as he had something important to say to them. He looked serious when he made the announcement, leaving them very puzzled. There had been no signs of the business failing, rather the contrary, and they could not think what else was so important. It was boiled beef sandwiches evening; every one turned up as well as the factory hands, including a couple of cousins. Conversation was sparse as they all waited for David to speak. When all the beef sandwiches were consumed, David cleared his throat and began.

"No doubt you'll all be shocked when I tell you I hope to get married soon." There were gasps of surprise and a look of joy on his mother's face.

"Mazeltov!" she cried.

"However, I don't think any of you will be pleased with my choice of bride. But I want you to know that nothing anyone will say will alter my mind. There is no other woman in the world for me." For once, the family was too stunned to speak, then a chorus of questions: Who could she be? Why had it kept it secret? Why should they want to object? He let the questions rain down on his head, then put his hand up to silence them.

"It's Laura, our ex-maid, I'm hoping to marry." Momma collapsed in the chair.

"Vot? Is my son a meshugena? I got a madman in the house! How come such a thing? She's not kosher, she's got nothing and she's too young already!"

"She's a sly one, making up to you under our noses" was a sister's comment.

"Don't you dare say that!" David snapped back. "Any chasing that has been done has been done by me. I won't have a word said against her."

"But why," Momma wailed, "didn't you let the Rabbi find you a nice Jewish girl? Laura is a shiksa."

"Laura is not a heathen; she believes in people and doesn't believe she's special because of a religion." David had to speak up for Laura. He continued, "Now tell me, Momma, and I want you to answer my questions truthfully, is Laura a hardworking girl?" A reluctant nod. "Is Laura an honest girl?" Another nod. "Is she good-tempered and well-behaved?" Nod. "Is she intelligent?" Nod. "And we all can see she is very beautiful. Now Momma, if I can marry an honest, hard-working, good-tempered, good-living, intelligent, beautiful wife, don't you think I shall be very lucky?"

"That's clever talk, but you should marry a nice Jewish girl from a good family. Also a maidel — Laura is used goods: Levy told me she has been married already! What would your father have thought? I don't agree to none of this." And she began to cry. The others mumbled their distress at this alarming turn of events.

David's heart sank. "Laura's brief marriage ended in tragedy, through no fault of her own," he explained. "Well, if none of you will recognise Laura as my wife when I marry I shall move away, but not too far for I'll keep the factory going as usual. I assume that will meet with your approval?" He left the room and went upstairs to his office. He was trembling.

The next day the atmosphere in the factory had changed. The boss had transgressed, but work must go on just the same. David wrote to Laura to assuage his heartache, telling her the family did not approve, but stating that his love for her was now even stronger. He spent all the spare time he could muster looking at houses and settled on a nice three-bedroomed semi-detached villa in Golders Green. Next he arranged for Laura to come to London for the weekend to choose furnishings and carpets, curtains and furniture. They did not go to shops, it was all from wholesalers. David was very pleased when he totted up how much they had saved.

"You old Shylock!" Laura teased him, but she felt life was impossibly good to her, although now and then she wept for Aden that his life had been so cruelly cut short. She remembered the period after his death feeling that her life had been ended too and there was no hope for any future happiness for her, and now she marvelled at how wonderfully everything had turned around for her. She felt she had not deserved it.

CHAPTER
THIRTEEN

Then the time came for the wedding. In her wedding suit and hat, radiant with happiness, she made a picture to gladden any eye. She bought her mother a new suit and David had one made for her father. The children stayed at an aunt's in the Forest for the day. They were not disappointed in not going to London since they knew presents would be bought for them. Laura's parents were very impressed and not really comfortable in the posh West End restaurant, and Laura's mother was open-mouthed with astonishment at the prices. Her parents were also very impressed at Laura's new home, in what was to them a grand house with modern cons such as they had never seen before.

Sex is a wonderful thing, and mixed with love it is magic, and so it was with David and Laura. But life is never perfect: there was the shadow of the family rift. Noticing a sadness in his face one evening Laura asked David if he regretted his actions, did he think he had sinned?

"Not against any god," he replied, "for I think gods are a man-imagined comfort in their dread of death. How can there be so many gods with special advantages for their followers? It doesn't make sense. Man is desperate for knowledge, but Laura, he has not found it. I feel however I have erred in my family's eyes and it grieves me, but maybe they will come round in time."

It was wonderful waking up in her new home in David's arms, but David did not object when Laura said she needed a part-time job to fill the hours. She found one in a boutique in Regent Street, where the prices were at first a shock to her. Sometimes the lady owner asked Laura to model gowns for customers. David was very proud of this. He appreciated Laura's intelligence and when they had some spare time he took her out to see London's treasures, such as the Tate Gallery and the National Gallery, where she marvelled at the skills of the artists. He remembered Laura's gift for drawing that had got Rachel in trouble at school. He bought her paints and brushes and an easel, and engaged a charwoman to clean their house so Laura could have time for her new hobby. He took her to the

British Museum, the Science Museum, the Victoria and Albert Museum, and to the theatres, and sometimes to a film in the West End. Life was almost like a fairy tale for Laura.

By the time they had been married for over a year, she became increasingly worried every time her monthly period came on. David longed above everything for a child. He went to the doctor for a check-up and found he had no medical problems. He dreaded to hurt Laura's feelings by discussing it but he too was very worried. Had the episode caused by his brother made her infertile? More grey hairs began to show on David's head. Then one month, when her period was six days overdue Laura went into a transport of hope. It made her so happy she looked more beautiful than ever. David became more bewitched with her. Then, to his dismay, she came out of the bathroom one bedtime and broke down, sobbing her heart out.

"What's the matter, darling?" begged a distraught David. It all came out: her bitter disappointment that she was not pregnant after all. She felt grief for David as well as herself. It took him some time to pacify her, after they wept together for their ill luck.

94

"Look, darling," David beseeched, "It may not be much the matter at all, sometimes nature takes its time. Anyway, if nothing happens during the next three months I'll take you to see the best gynaecologist in Harley Street." Comforted, they went to bed and found solace in each other's arms.

A few weeks later Laura woke up to the cup of tea David brought to her in the morning. She felt weirdly nauseous and the tea, usually so welcome, tasted like undrinkable poison. The thought of cooking scrambled eggs for breakfast was unbearable. She remembered the cream pastry they had bought with their elevenses coffee at the shop: maybe that had done it. She told David how she felt.

"Well, I'll call your shop from my office and let them know you won't be in today." he suggested.

"No," Laura objected, "Don't do that. Being at work will be better than being on my own. Besides, I want to see if the cakes have affected the girls at work too." For breakfast all she could face was some lemon juice in a glass of water and a bit of dried toast. At the shop, her employer and the other assistant both commented on Laura's pallor. They were both fine, so it was not the cake, as Laura suggested.

"Have you missed a period?" Phyllis, the assistant asked.

"Well, I'm about due now." Laura replied.

"I reckon you've a baby on the way. You're like me; one of the unlucky ones. I was sick and ill for the first months of both mine, but they were fine when they were born." To Phyllis's surprise she got a warm hug and kiss from Laura.

"Oh, if only you're right! I don't mind how ill I feel if it's due to a baby!"

The awful nausea continued and the abhorrence for all her usual diet. Sometimes she only wanted green sour apples or dry porridge oats. David insisted she go to the doctor, who warned them that it was very early days to be sure, but the condition did happen in the early weeks of pregnancy to some unlucky women.

Unlucky! Laura felt she was the luckiest person in the world. On the way home she confessed with some embarrassment that she fancied a glass of cider. "And a glass of cider you shall have, my darling," David said, "or wouldn't you rather it was champagne?"

The sickness carried on well into her fourth month. She grew thin and pale, despite David getting her anything, however odd, that she fancied to eat. The grey hairs at his temples became noticeable. Then almost overnight the nausea went, but her appetite remained odd. She left work and busied herself preparing for the baby, knitting and sewing and shopping for baby things. Joy oozed out of their pores. David longed to shout his good news to the world, especially to his mother and family, but the thought of their disapproval was more than he could emotionally risk. Nevertheless, they noticed his good humour, putting it down to the business doing well.

It was arranged for Laura's mother to come up to London for a week to help when Laura brought the baby home. Her aunt was going to take care of her siblings. Still, the loneliness of her lot saddened Laura slightly. Her elderly Jewish neighbours did not want to mix with a young shiksa wife. Then one day in the street, an arm came round her and there was Dolly! "Oh Dolly, how glad I am to see you" Laura exclaimed. "Where are you going?"

"To the pictures," was the reply. "I've come this way because they're showing a Clark Gable picture. I'm mad about him."

"I wish you could come home with me and have a meal with us and I could show you my baby things." Laura invited her.

"Of course I will," Dolly replied, "Clark Gable won't miss me. But are you sure Mr. David won't mind?" she added.

"Oh Dolly, he's wonderful to me. He'd give me the moon if he could reach it." Laura gushed.

"Well, he's certainly given you something that makes you look like a moon!" Dolly indicated Laura's bulge. "When is it due?"

"In the next two weeks. Do you think any of David's family know?" Laura asked.

"I'm sure they don't or I would have heard about it. I had a row at work and nearly left the job when you got married. They seemed to think he had committed a mortal sin. I told them protestant girls were just as good as Jewish ones — they only think they are better off 'cause their dads are better at making money than ours are."

They had a lovely cosy evening. Before David came home Laura made a pot of tea and the two old friends had a long chat, sat by the kitchen table.

"Do you mind me asking about your previous marriage?" Dolly asked. "You only wrote me a short letter to say your husband had been killed. What happened?"

Laura discovered that now she could talk about it without emotion. "It's such a relief to talk to someone about it, you've no idea! I've never really discussed it with David. Aden was a good man, a wonderful husband and was very fond of me, but all the time we were together I felt guilty since I couldn't love him as I should; my thoughts were never off "Mr. David", and that's not a good basis for a marriage."

"Didn't he want any children?" Dolly asked.

"Oh, we hadn't been that long married, and I wasn't sure I could have any, after the abortion. It was something we were going to discuss later on. But of course, that never came. Oh Dolly, I felt so guilty when he was killed! I was never the wife I should have been to him. It's so different now with David! But for ages I felt his death was some kind of punishment to me for not loving him enough. I had so many hopes of our future together, and that in time I would forget about David and make Aden happy, but that cave-in at the pit put an end to it. At one low point after the funeral I really thought I could never be happy again. And do you know, now I never even think of him. Dolly, do you think it wrong for me to have forgotten Aden, and be this happy? I don't really deserve it."

Dolly gave her the answer she wanted to hear, and after Laura gave her a hug she helped her get the dinner ready for three. When he returned from work, David was glad for Laura to have Dolly's company and he smiled as the women drooled over the baby things. Laura told Dolly she would be very grateful to see her whenever she could spare some of her free time.

CHAPTER
FOURTEEN

A few days later at about midnight Laura woke with contractions, which after a time became severe, and she allowed David to call a taxi. Her case was already packed and the journey to the hospital took only a few minutes. The driver wished them all the luck and David, half mad with worry and half mad with joy, handed Laura over to the nurses. The look of agony on her face almost made him want to turn the clock back. He went into the small, comfortable waiting room, mopping his sweating face as he walked up and down and tried to look at one of the magazines. A nurse came in and said, "Why don't you go home and try to get some sleep? It's a first baby and could take some time." But wild horses would not drag David away until Laura's agony was over. After a while the nurse brought a cup of tea and a biscuit.

"All is taking its normal course: it won't be much longer." she assured him. He was glad of the tea for his stomach ached and he felt quite ill. A quarter of an hour later he was a new man, pain gone, feeling on top of the world when the nurse came to tell him he had a fine 8lb 2 oz son. He hugged her in his joy and followed her into the ward. There, washed and groomed, in a pretty nightie and bed jacket, eyes shining with adoration at the beautiful baby in her arms, was proud Laura. The picture almost took David's breath away. There were tears of joy in his eyes and a great feeling of thanks in his heart.

The first thing in the morning he sent a telegram to Laura's parents and his workforce were surprised to get a bonus each in their pay packets. They assumed it must be conscience money for betraying his faith.

The baby thrived and was an object of adoration for Laura's mother whilst she was there. Dolly too fussed over him, but David's heart ached for his mother and family to be with him. Although he enjoyed supreme happiness in his marriage, there were times when the black clouds of depression engulfed him. He badly missed going down to the cosy kitchen at Leman Street for his meal after work when he and his siblings would laugh and argue and gently exchange ideas on many subjects, apart from the business. And he missed his mother's adoration of him. Sometimes he felt the full shock of his unorthodox behaviour, but he could not regret his marriage.

He had broken the spiritual bond of the family; but he argued to himself it was an ephemeral bond built on myths. Human beings, he reasoned, must have come from a common source. No just god would choose one section, e.g. the Jewish race, as the chosen tribe. Such a myth, he reckoned, caused a good deal of anti-Semitism. Human egotism had created many gods, and the problems that went with them. His familiar attitude of withdrawn coolness belittled him as a person.

When the baby was three months old, it became unendurable. So one day, when having his elevenses in the kitchen at Leman Street, he asked his mother if she still had any love for him.

"Of course I do!" she exclaimed, and burst into tears.

"Well, will you do me a big favour? There is someone at my house that very much wants to meet you," David replied.

"You mean Laura?" Momma assumed.

"No, I don't mean Laura, it isn't a woman."

"Not a woman!" his mother was puzzled. "Vot man vont to see me? Is it to do with the business?"

"Yes, it's very much much to do with business." David replied.

"Then I'll come," she consented, "But I don't understand. I know nothing about business. Shall I wear my best clothes?"

"No, come in whatever makes you comfortable. I'll take you home Friday evening, so you don't have to cook then."

He hired a taxi and, on arriving at his house, Momma was very impressed with the house in Golders Green. The door-knocker was brilliantly polished while the whole front had a well-kept air. She thought to herself that Laura was a worker, there was no doubt about that. David hung up her coat and hat and ushered her into the lounge, leaving her there while he went to find Laura. She looked around for the man she had to meet, but there was no-one there. Then she spotted a cradle on legs by the fire. There was a squeal of delight.

"Oh my beauty! My precious! My darlink!" and the baby that had been trying to put a toe in his mouth was swept up into his granny's arms. He was indeed a lovely baby, and to his grandmomma's delight his great brown eyes and physiognomy showed traces of his Jewish ancestry.

David came back into the room, "You pleased you met this young man, then?" he asked his mother.

"Oh, David!" She put her arm out to bend his head for a kiss.

"Why didn't you tell me? I'm so happy!"

At that moment, Laura came in with coffee and sandwiches. She put the tray down and went over to kiss the top of Momma's grey head and she was not repulsed. The twain had met.

The next Friday it was a full house at Leman Street with enough salt beef sandwiches and dill pickles for everyone, including David and Laura. All the women enjoyed a cuddle with the baby and unanimously declared him the loveliest baby in the world, and the image of his father. The little ambassador of all this good will gurgled and slept his way through all the fuss.

David Bailey Cohen grew up to be the greatly revered humanist philosopher.

Also available in ISIS Large Print:

Searching for Tilly

Susan Sallis

A touching story of love, loss and discovery

Three women came to the remote Cornish cottage that summer: Jenna, only 26 and grieving for the loss of the love of her life; her mother Caro, whose husband Steve had also died; and Laura, who had been married to Caro's beloved brother Geoff. The house where they were staying was called The Widow's Cottage, and it was poignantly suitable.

In that tiny Cornish community, the three discover strange memories of their forebears, and especially of Tilly, Cora's mother. They become swept up in the story of Tilly and her family - a story that takes them on an epic journey across the West Country and to the solution of an amazing family mystery.

ISBN 978-0-7531-7952-9 (hb)
ISBN 978-0-7531-7953-6 (pb)

Out of this Nettle

Norah Lofts

His name was Colin Lowrie. A tall, red-haired Scot; a man at 16, whose pride was the ancient clan pride of the Lowries.

And when the clans were broken — massacred in a brutal revenge at Culloden Field — Colin Lowrie was forced to take flight on a journey half-way round the world. A journey to a barbaric slave plantation in the West Indies, then on to New Orleans and a life of lust and debauchery — and to a strange eerie love affair with an eccentric heiress . . .

And always, wherever destiny or chance took the young Scottish rebel, he carried with him the dream of Braidlowrie — Braidlowrie, the home of the Lowries — the home from which he was forever exiled . . .

ISBN 978-0-7531-7940-6 (hb)
ISBN 978-0-7531-7941-3 (pb)

Peter West

D. E. Stevenson

Beth Kerr is the daughter of the boatman in the small village of Kintoul. Her mother died at an early age, after an unhappy marriage that caused her family to cast her aside. As the years pass, Beth grows into a beautiful young woman, watched over by the quiet Peter West. The owner of Kintoul House, Peter is a lonely man with a weak heart and few family members and friends. They both struggle with their feelings for one another, before being forced to embark on marriages decided upon by their families. But will their lives follow the paths set for them, or will they find their own way?

ISBN 978-0-7531-7824-9 (hb)
ISBN 978-0-7531-7825-6 (pb)

To Kill For Love

Winifred Foley

The village chapel has no graveyard; villagers must go to rest in the churchyard two miles away. Many of the graves have headstones and those that haven't are neatly trimmed and in season have their jam-jars of flowers, but in a corner there's one grave with an unreadable headstone, overgrown with weeds and the grass never tended. A wild rose has seeded itself there and tries to ramble over the neglect. The identity of the remains that lie beneath are often pondered by those with romantic ideas.

Another of Winifred Foley's inimitable stories of life, death and love set in the Forest of Dean. She traces the lives of two generations who are touched with tragedy, but also raised by the heights of selfless love.

ISBN 978-0-7531-7654-2 (hb)
ISBN 978-0-7531-7655-9 (pb)

Dreamscapes

Tamara McKinley

Catriona Summers' debut in show business came early.
When she was barely minutes old, her father, the leader
of a travelling music hall troupe that toured the small
towns of the Outback, carried her on stage in order to
introduce her to her first audience.

From such humble beginnings Catriona had grown up
to emerge as a rare talent, her voice garnering her
praise from the public and critics alike. But her journey
from performing popular songs for a few pennies to
becoming an accliamed opera diva on the Sydney stage,
was fraught with hardship and tragedy. And now some
old scandalous secrets from her teenage years are
threatening her present, her family and all she has
achieved . . .

ISBN 978-0-7531-7529-3 (hb)
ISBN 978-0-7531-7530-9 (pb)

ISIS publish a wide range of books in large print, from fiction to biography. Any suggestions for books you would like to see in large print or audio are always welcome. Please send to the Editorial Department at:

ISIS Publishing Limited
7 Centremead
Osney Mead
Oxford OX2 0ES

A full list of titles is available free of charge from:

Ulverscroft Large Print Books Limited

(UK)
The Green
Bradgate Road, Anstey
Leicester LE7 7FU
Tel: (0116) 236 4325

(Australia)
P.O. Box 314
St Leonards
NSW 1590
Tel: (02) 9436 2622

(USA)
P.O. Box 1230
West Seneca
N.Y. 14224-1230
Tel: (716) 674 4270

(Canada)
P.O. Box 80038
Burlington
Ontario L7L 6B1
Tel: (905) 637 8734

(New Zealand)
P.O. Box 456
Feilding
Tel: (06) 323 6828

Details of **ISIS** complete and unabridged audio books are also available from these offices. Alternatively, contact your local library for details of their collection of **ISIS** large print and unabridged audio books.